GERALD McBOING BOING

based on the Academy Award®–winning motion picture by

Dr. Seuss

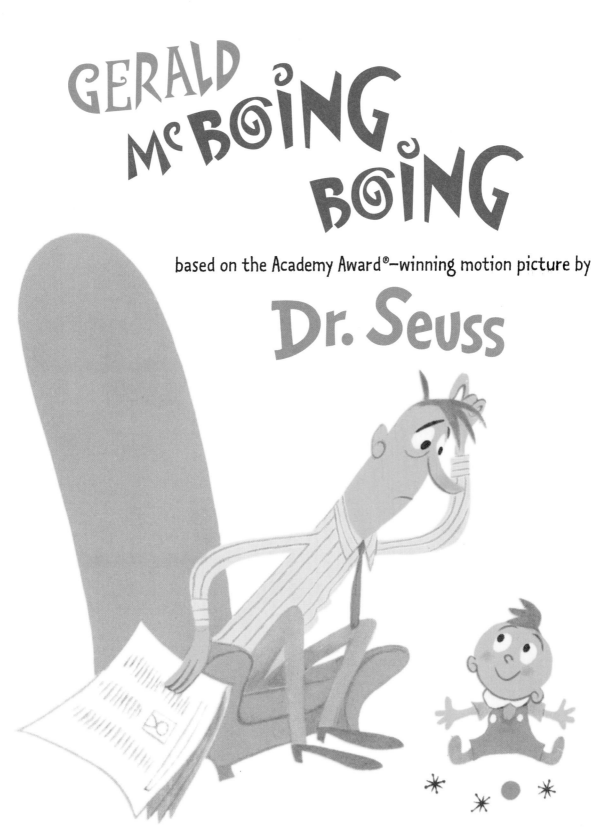

pictures adapted by MEL CRAWFORD

Random House 🏠 New York

Based on the movie *Gerald McBoing Boing,* copyright © 1950,
renewed 1978 by Columbia Pictures Industries, Inc.

Published in the United States by Random House Children's Books,
a division of Penguin Random House LLC, New York. Originally published
in a different form by Random House Children's Books, in 2000.

Random House and the colophon are registered trademarks of
Penguin Random House LLC.

Visit us on the Web!
Seussville.com
randomhousekids.com

Educators and librarians, for a variety of teaching tools, visit us at
RHTeachersLibrarians.com

ISBN 978-1-5247-1635-6 (trade) — ISBN 978-1-5247-1757-5 (lib. bdg.)

Library of Congress Catalog Card Number: 99-067111

Printed in the United States of America
10 9 8 7 6 5 4 3 2

This is the story of Gerald McCloy
And the strange thing that happened
to that little boy.

They say it all started
when Gerald was two.
That's the age kids start talking—
least, most of them do.
Well, when he started talking,
you know what he said?

He didn't talk words—
    he went BOING BOING! instead!
"What's that?" cried his father,
    his face turning gray.
"That's a very odd thing
    for a young boy to say!"

And poor Gerald's father
    rushed to the phone
And quick dialed the number
    of Doctor Malone.
"Come over fast!"
    the poor father pled.
"Our boy can't speak words—
    he goes BOING BOING instead!"

"I see," said the doctor.
"It's just as you said.
He doesn't speak words—
he goes BOING BOING instead!

"I've no cure for this.
I can't handle the case."
And he packed up his pills
and walked out of the place.

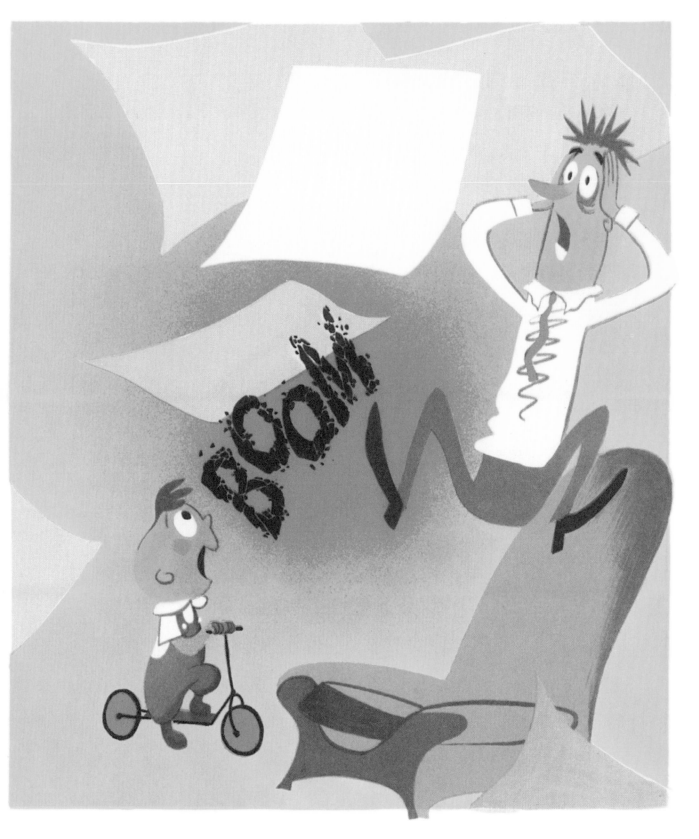

Then months passed, and Gerald
got louder and louder
Till one day he went *BOOM!*
like a big keg of powder!

It was then that his father
  said, "This is enough!
He'll drive us both mad
  with this terrible stuff!
A boy of his age
  shouldn't sound like a fool.
He's got to learn words.
  We must send him to school."

So Gerald marched off,
an obedient creature.

But he soon was back home
with a note from the teacher.
"From Public School Seven
to Mrs. McCloy:

Your little son Gerald's
a most hopeless boy.
We cannot accept him,
for we have a rule
That pupils must not go
Cuckoo in our school.
Your boy will go HONK
all his life, I'm afraid.
Sincerely yours, Fanny Schultz,
Teacher, First Grade."

And as little Gerald
    grew older, he found
When a fellow goes BAM!
    no one wants him around.

When a fellow goes *SKREEK!*
he won't have any friends.
For once he says, *"CLANG CLANG CLANG!"*
all the fun ends.

"Nyah nyah!" they all shouted,
"Your name's not McCloy!
You're Gerald McBoing Boing,
the noise-making boy!"

Poor Gerald decided
that he had no place
At home, in the school—
in the whole human race!

And so he concluded
that, drear and forlorn,
He would just disappear
in the thick of a storm.

But as he was boarding
a slow-moving freight,
A voice from the darkness
called out, "Stop, boy! Wait!"

"Aren't you Gerald McBoing Boing,
  the lad who makes squeaks?
My boy, I have searched
  for you many long weeks!
I can make you the most
  famous lad in the nation,
For I own the BONG-BONG-BONG
  Radio Station!

"I need a smart fellow
to make all the sounds,
Who can **bark** like a dog,
and **bay** like the hounds!

"Your GONG is terrific,
your toot is inspired!
Quick come to BONG-BONG-BONG,
McBoing Boing—you're hired!"

Now his parents, proud parents,
   are able to boast
That their Gerald's CLOP-CLOP, BANG!
   is known coast to coast.

Now Gerald is rich,
    he has friends, he's well fed,
'Cause he doesn't speak words—
    he goes BOING BOING instead!